Library of Congress Cataloging-in-Publication Data

Korman, Justine.
To fly with dragons / by Justine and Ron Fontes; illustrated by Ted Enik.
p.   cm.
SUMMARY: After moving to a new house, Max and Emmy discover a secret drawer
containing a dragon scale that magically transports them to Dragon Land.
ISBN 0-375-80661-X   [1. Brothers and sisters—Fiction.   2. Dragons—Fiction.
3. Magic—Fiction.]
I. Fontes, Ron.   II. Enik, Ted; ill.   III. Title.   PZ7.K83692 To 2000   99-086026

www.randomhouse.com/kids/sesame

Visit Dragon Tales on the Web at www.dragontales.com

Printed in Italy   October 2000   10 9 8 7 6 5 4 3 2 1

To Fly with Dragons

I wish, I wish
With all my heart
To fly with dragons
In a land apart.

Adapted by Justine and Ron Fontes
From a script by Cliff Ruby and Elana Lesser
Based on the characters by Ron Rodecker
Illustrated by Ted Enik

Sesame Workshop / Random House

The magic began the moment Emmy and Max first set eyes on their new house—they just didn't know it yet.

"I hate it already!" Max grumbled as he marched up the front steps. "I don't want to live here!"

"Come on, Max, it won't be so bad," Emmy said, using her cheeriest big-sister voice. "Remember, it's *home* now."

But even Emmy's voice trembled just a little.

"Why don't you wait until you see inside before you make up your minds," their mother said as she opened the front door.

Their father gave them a gentle push. "Try the door at the top of the stairs," he said. "Look for the dragon."

Look for the dragon? What could he mean?

The children walked into the house, looking around at doors and windows and hallways they'd never seen before. The dragon was easy to spot. Max blinked. The friendly-looking dragon seemed to wink at him!

Emmy opened the door slowly—to find an amazing playroom!
"Look! Our toys are here!" Max squealed with delight.
Max grabbed his green dump truck and plopped himself in the
window seat. He swung his legs happily as he spun the wheels.
One shoe hit the seat with a loud *thud*!

"Oh, no," Max whispered, looking down at a big crack in the wood. "Emmy, I broke the new house!"

"You didn't break it," Emmy said, taking a closer look. She wiggled her fingers into the crack and pulled. "It's a secret drawer!"

A lovely glow, like starlight, was coming from inside the drawer. But the only thing inside was a small box.

"Let me!" Max cried, opening the lid. Inside, a strange something glowed with rainbow colors. Emmy looked at the box, then at the dragons on the wall. She knew at once what the something was.

"It's a dragon scale, Max," Emmy said in an excited whisper. "And look what's written on the box."

Together, they read the rhyme aloud:

"I wish, I wish
With all my heart
To fly with dragons
In a land apart."

As the children spoke, dragons leapt off the wallpaper and began to dance in the air. The dragons whirled faster and faster around them. The walls of the playroom seemed to melt away.

The next thing the children knew, they were standing in the middle of a wide green meadow. The playroom, the dragon scale, and the sparkles had vanished.

"Where are we, Emmy?" Max gasped. "I want to go home!"

Emmy reached down to see if the meadow was real or just a dream. At the touch of her finger, a rock turned from dull brown to brilliant blue!

"Look at this!" Emmy held the rock up for Max to see.

"I found a rock, too," Max said as he picked up a triangle-shaped stone. But it just stayed white. "Figures," Max grumbled, stuffing it into his pocket.

"Max, I think the dragon scale took us someplace magical!" Emmy said, beaming.

The children were so busy looking at all the wonders around them that they never even thought to look up.

They *did* notice, though, when two creatures swooped down from the clouds and landed with a THUMP!

"Emmy!" Max cried, hiding behind his sister. *"Dragons!"*

"You won't bite me, will you?" the big blue dragon asked nervously. He tried to hide, too.

"Me bite *you?"* Max said, his fear fading with a giggle.

"I'm Emmy and this is Max," Emmy told the dragons.

"I'm Cassie," the pink dragon answered shyly. "And this is my friend Ord."

"Where are we?" Emmy wondered out loud.

"Dragon Land!" Cassie replied. "I've never seen real children here before." Suddenly, there came a thundering rumble. It was Ord's tummy.

"Time for a snack!" Ord tossed up some purple popcorn kernels—and popped them in the air with a burst of fire breath!

"Now I'm not hungry anymore…just sad," Ord said with a sigh. He explained that he had lost his first baby tooth that morning and couldn't find it anywhere.

"Why don't you check all the places you played today?" Emmy suggested. "That's what I do when I lose things."

"Maybe I lost my tooth at Singing Springs when I showed it to Zak and Wheezie," Ord said, thinking out loud. "Come on, let's fly!"

With a great bound, both dragons took to the sky.

"Aren't you coming?" Ord asked with a puzzled look.

Emmy was embarrassed to admit that children couldn't fly.

"Can't fly?!" Ord said, amazed.

"Do you want a ride?" Cassie asked.

Emmy didn't have to think twice. "Definitely!" she shouted.

Then Emmy and Max *were* flying—soaring high above the meadow on the backs of two dragons.

"Wheeeee!" Max shrieked in glee.

Soon the dragons came in for a landing near a cave.

Suddenly, there was a loud rumble—but this time it wasn't Ord's stomach. The ground quaked, and a gaping black hole appeared.

"What's *that?*" Emmy asked in alarm.

"Haven't you ever seen a knuckerhole before?" Ord asked the startled children. Before he could explain, a two-headed dragon exploded out of the hole. WHOOSH!

"I said we should have turned *right!*" snapped the purple half.

"Well, I got us here, didn't I?" whined the green half. "It just took longer."

"These are our friends Zak and Wheezie," Cassie told the children, giggling at their surprised faces.

"Real children?" Wheezie gasped. "Loooooove it!"

"Wheezie! Stop yelling in my ear!" Zak complained.

"Oh, stop being such a fuddy-duddy!" Wheezie scolded.

Ord interrupted the squabbling by asking, "Have you two seen my tooth?"

Zak and Wheezie shook their heads.

"Um…what about Quetzal?" Cassie suggested shyly. "Maybe he can help."

"What's a Quetzal?" Max wondered.

"He's our teacher at the School in the Sky," Ord explained. "Quetzal will know what to do. He knows everything!"

With a flutter of wings, they were all on their way! Soon they caught their first glimpse of the school, high on a mountain.

A large golden dragon came out to meet them. *"¡Qué sorpresa!* Children!" he exclaimed. *"¡Hola, niños!"*

"You speak Spanish," Emmy said in amazement.

"Sí, I come from Mexico," Quetzal explained. Max and Emmy couldn't believe it—their family was from Mexico, too!

"What a surprise to see children in Dragon Land once more," Quetzal said, beaming.

Once more? Emmy thought to herself. But before she could ask, Quetzal gestured for everyone to come inside.

The old teacher pulled down a book from a shelf. He waved his great claws and the book opened by itself! Emmy and Max watched in wonder as pictures floated off the page.

"You see, *niños,* long ago there was a lonely dragon
who wished to play with children," Quetzal read.
"So she sprinkled magic dust on her brightest,
shiniest scales and blew them right
out of Dragon Land."

From the page
rose the picture
of a rainbow-
colored scale.
"It's just like
ours back
home!" Max cried.
"Whenever children
are lucky enough to find a scale, they
come to visit Dragon Land," Quetzal
said, finishing his story. He closed
the big book.

Ord had been listening carefully, but now he remembered something else. "We still haven't found my tooth!" he sniffled.

Max suddenly remembered something, too. He dug into his pocket and pulled out the white stone he'd found.

"Is *this* your tooth?" Max said, holding it out to Ord.

"Max! You found it!" Ord exclaimed, scooping the boy up in a hug. "Dragons get a wish for every tooth that falls out. Now I can make one!"

"What will you wish for?" Max wanted to know.

Ord smiled. "I'll wish that you could play with us all the time!" He blew on the tooth to make his wish.

"Looooove it!" Wheezie squealed.

Emmy definitely liked the idea of playing with the dragons, but she was starting to miss her parents and her home. Their house might be new, but it *was* home after all.

"I'd like to visit again, but right now I wish we could go home," Emmy said. "Only we don't know *how!*"

Quetzal smiled. "Do not worry, *niña*," he said.

Quetzal's eyes twinkled. "There is a way to make both wishes come true." He handed each of the dragons their own magic scale.

"When you rub these scales," Quetzal told them, "Max and Emmy's scale will glow, telling them to come play." And Max and Emmy could use their own scale to make the journey back to Dragon Land—anytime they wanted!

"As for you, *niños,*" Quetzal told Emmy and Max, "here is a rhyme to send you home."

The children said it after him, word for word:

"I wish, I wish
To use this rhyme
To go back home
Until next time!"

In a flash, the children were back in their playroom. The clock on the wall showed that no time had passed. They ran to find their dragon scale to make sure it hadn't been just a dream. Sure enough, the scale was there, snug in its box.

From the hallway, they heard their mother call, "Emmy! Max! How do you like our new home?"

Emmy didn't know what to say.

Max did. It turned out to be the perfect answer.

"Loooooove it!"